ANANSI and the MAGIC STICK

by ERIC A. KIMMEL

illustrated by JANET STEVENS

HOLIDAY HOUSE
New York

It was a fine bright day. All the animals were

working

        working

                working

in their gardens. All except Anansi the Spider.
Anansi lay in his front yard, fast asleep.

Warthog, Lion, and Zebra came walking by. "Look at Anansi! He is so lazy!" said Zebra. "His house is falling apart. His yard is full of trash. He wouldn't get out of bed if his house caught fire."

"Anansi is so lazy, he falls asleep standing up," said Lion.

"He is so lazy, moss grows on his head," Warthog added.

Their noisy laughter woke Anansi. "Be quiet! I am not lazy at all. I am thinking. My mind is working hard." Anansi tapped his forehead.

The animals laughed even harder.

Anansi walked away. "I don't have to listen to you. I'll find another place to sleep—I mean, *think*!"

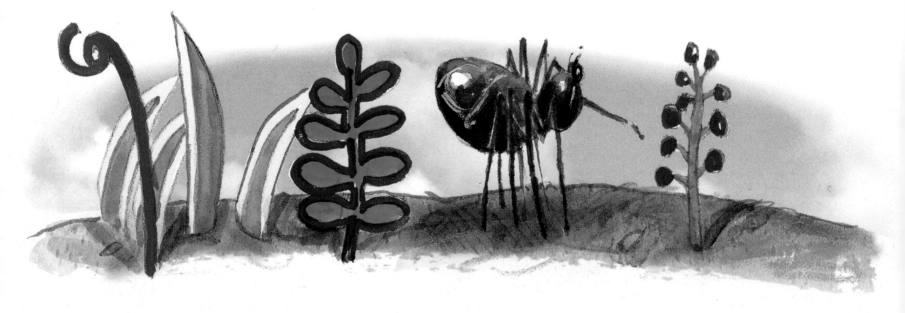

Anansi started **walking**
                              walking
                                            walking down the road. Before he knew it,
he had walked all the way to Hyena's house. Hyena lay in his hammock,
fast asleep. His house was neat and tidy. His yard was beautifully planted
with shrubs and flowers.

"What is Hyena's secret?" Anansi wondered. "No one ever sees him working. Yet his house always looks beautiful. I need to find out how he does it."

Anansi hid behind a bush, watching and waiting.

Hyena woke up. He noticed a pile of dust on the path. He spoke to a stick leaning against a post:

Hocus-pocus, Magic Stick.
Sweep this dust up.
Quick, quick, quick!

As Anansi watched, the magic stick swept away the dust.

When the dust was gone, Hyena said,
"Abra-Canabra-Cadabra!"
Down fell the stick!

Hyena leaned it back against the
post and went inside his house.
    "That's just what I need!" said Anansi.
"If I had that magic stick, my house
would be as beautiful as Hyena's. No
one would laugh at me again!"
    Anansi grabbed the magic stick and
ran off as fast as his legs could go.

He soon became tired. "Why am I carrying this stick? It can carry me!" Anansi said the magic words, just as he remembered them:

Hocus-pocus, Magic Stick.
Carry me home now.
Quick, quick, quick!

The stick picked up Anansi and carried him along. When they arrived at Anansi's house, he said, *"Abra-Canabra-Cadabra!"*

KPOM! The magic stick dropped Anansi on his head. "Ow!" Anansi cried. "Next time put me down gently, Stick! There's lots of work to do. Get rid of this trash first."

Anansi said the magic words:

Hocus-pocus, Magic Stick.
Clean my yard up.
Quick, quick, quick!

The magic stick whirled round and round. It gathered all the trash and threw it over the fence into Lion's yard.

"Abra-Canabra-Cadabra!"
Down fell the stick!

"Good job, Stick! Next my house."

Hocus-pocus, Magic Stick.
Fix my house up.
Quick, quick, quick!

The magic stick whirled round and round. Wood and nails flew through the air. Bright pink paint splashed over the fence as Zebra came walking by. Anansi's house gleamed.

So did Zebra. He was bright pink, too!

"Abra-Canabra-Cadabra!"
Down fell the stick!

"Now for my garden,"
Anansi said.

Hocus-pocus, Magic Stick.
Plant and water.
Quick, quick, quick!

The magic stick whirled round and round. It dug up the dirt, throwing the weeds into Warthog's tomato patch.

It planted seeds in neat, straight rows. Then it began to water them.

Anansi yawned. "Watching all this work makes me tired. I need a nap. Keep watering, Stick! Don't stop!"

Anansi lay down and went to sleep.

The magic stick kept **watering**

watering

watering.

The vegetables grew **bigger**
bigger
bigger.

The water flowed across Anansi's yard and out the gate:
a trickle at first, then a stream,

then a flood,

then a mighty river.

"HELP!" the animals cried.

"Help!" cried Anansi, waking up to find himself afloat in the middle of a raging river. He tried to make the water stop, but he couldn't remember the magic words.

"*Canabra-Catabra-Cadabra?*"

"*Calabra-Cazabra-Cavabra?*"

"*Cajabra-Camabra-Capabra?*"

Nothing happened. The water kept flowing. **"Help!"** cried Anansi.

Hyena came drifting by.

"Hello, Anansi," he said. "It's a nice day to be on the water. By the way, I'm looking for a magic stick. Have you seen it?"

"A funny-looking stick just came floating by," Anansi said. "I can't see it now. It must be underwater. I think Crocodile ate it."

"Or else he's using it as a toothpick. I better get it back before he breaks it." Hyena leaned over the water and said:

Hocus-pocus, Magic Stick.
No more magic.
End of trick!

Abra-Canabra-Cadabra!

The river stopped flowing, leaving behind a wide lake. "What are you going to do about this lake?" the animals asked.

"There's nothing I can do," Hyena said. "The lake is here, and here it stays. You'll have to learn to enjoy it."

So they did. The animals built new homes on the lakeshore. They swam, jumped, and played in the bright blue water.

But someone was missing. Where was Anansi? Did the flood sweep him away? Did he tumble over a waterfall?

"Poor Anansi!" the animals sniffled, wiping away their tears. "We'll never see him again."

They were wrong! Anansi was far away on the other side of the lake, floating along in his new houseboat, sleeping all day, and **planning**

new

tricks,

which is just what Anansi does best.

AUTHOR'S NOTE

Anansi and the Magic Stick is loosely based on a
Liberian story called *The Magic Hoe*. Readers will
no doubt see similarities to the story of
The Sorcerer's Apprentice. Magic that gets out
of control is a common theme in all cultures!

To Mickey
E. A. K.

To Eric,
We could have used
a magic stick....
J. S.

Text copyright © 2001 by Eric A. Kimmel
Illustrations copyright © 2001 by Janet Stevens
All Rights Reserved
Printed in the United States of America
The text typeface is Fritz.
The artwork was created using digital elements, watercolor, watercolor
crayon, and acrylic on 300 pound Lanaquarelle watercolor paper.
www.holidayhouse.com

Library of Congress Cataloging-in-Publication Data
Kimmel, Eric A.
Anansi and the magic stick / retold by Eric A. Kimmel;
illustrated by Janet Stevens.—1st ed.
p. cm.
Summary: Anansi the Spider steals Hyena's magic stick
so he won't have to do the chores, but when the stick's magic won't stop,
he gets more than he bargained for.
ISBN 0-8234-1443-4 (hardcover)   ISBN: 0-8234-1763-8 (paperback)
1. Anansi (Legendary character)—Legends.
[1. Anansi (Legendary character)—Legends. 2. Folklore—Africa, West.]
I. Stevens, Janet, ill. Title.
PZ8.1.K567 An 2001
398.24'52544—dc21 [E] 00-039608

ISBN-13: 978-0-8234-1443-7 (hardcover)   ISBN-10: 0-8234-1443-4 (hardcover)
ISBN-13: 978-0-8234-1763-6 (paperback)   ISBN-10: 0-8234-1763-8 (paperback)